THE GIANT CABBAGE

AN ALASKA FOLKTALE

CHÉRIE B. STIHLER

ILLUSTRATED BY JEREMIAH TRAMMELL

PAWS IV
PUBLISHED BY SASQUATCH BOOKS

Chérie Stihler and her husband, Scott, have made Fairbanks their home since 1996. She is an elementary educator and a member of the Society of Children's Book Writers and Illustrators. This is her first book.

Jeremiah Trammell is a lifelong Alaskan who recently moved to Seattle, Washington. His paintings have been published in magazines, prints, and greeting cards. This is his first book.

This is dedicated to the most wonderful man in the world—my husband, my best friend—Scott Stihler. And for my former students in Oakland, California: Here is the first "Alaska Story" I promised you. Hugs and such—Mrs. Stihler.
—C. S.

I would like to dedicate this to Isaac, Simon, Andy, and Jennifer.
—J. T.

Text copyright ©2003 by Chérie B. Stihler
Illustrations copyright ©2003 by Jeremiah Trammell

Published by Sasquatch Books
Printed in China
Distributed by Publishers Group West
09 08 07 06 05 04 03   6 5 4 3 2

Cover design and art direction: Karen Schober
Interior design: Elizabeth Cromwell

Library of Congress Cataloging in Publication Data
Stihler, Chérie B.
    The giant cabbage: an Alaska folktale / by Chérie B. Stihler ; illustrated by Jeremiah Trammel
        p. cm.
    Summary: Moose grows an enormous cabbage, sure to win a prize at the fair, but needs
    the help of all his friends to load it onto a truck in this Alaskan version of a Russian folktale.
    ISBN-157061-357-5
    [1. Folklore—Russia] I. Trammel, Jeremiah, ill. II. Title
PZ8.1.S85745Gi 2003
398.2'0947—dc21
[E]   2002191179

Sasquatch Books
119 South Main Street, Suite 400
Seattle, Washington 98104
206/467-4300
www.sasquatchbooks.com
books@sasquatchbooks.com

Moose looked out at his wonderful garden.
He had rows and rows of tasty vegetables.

"The fair starts this week. I need to find my best cabbage
for the Giant Cabbage Contest." The vegetables had all
grown very large under the Midnight Sun.

Then he saw it. It was a **big** cabbage.

It was a **really big** cabbage.

It was the **biggest** cabbage he had ever seen.

"It's **huge!** It's **enormous!**" Moose marveled.

"Why, this is a GIANT cabbage.
This is sure to win a prize at the fair!"

Moose trimmed the cabbage from the plant.

He tried to lift the cabbage and load it onto the truck.

He pushed and he tugged.

He bumped and he shoved.

But the cabbage did not move.

It did not even budge.

Just then Bear waved hello as she pedaled home from the library.

"Please come help me load this cabbage," yelled Moose.

Bear came right over. She saw the cabbage. It was a **big** cabbage. It was a **really big** cabbage. It was the **biggest** cabbage she had ever seen. "It's **huge!** It's **enormous!**" Bear growled. "Why, this is a GIANT cabbage! This is sure to win a prize at the fair!"

"I cannot lift this cabbage alone," said Moose.

"I will help you," promised Bear.

Moose grabbed hold of the cabbage.

Bear grabbed hold of the cabbage.

They pushed and they tugged.

They bumped and they shoved.

But the cabbage did not move.

It did not even budge.

Wolf trotted by Moose's garden on his way to the post office and saw the cabbage.

It was a **big** cabbage. It was a **really big** cabbage. It was the **biggest** cabbage he had ever seen. "It's **huge!** It's **enormous!**" Wolf howled. "Why, this is a GIANT cabbage! This is sure to win a prize at the fair!"

"We cannot lift this cabbage alone," said Moose. "I will help you," promised Wolf.

Moose grabbed hold of the cabbage. Bear grabbed hold of Moose. Wolf grabbed hold of Bear.

They pushed and they tugged.

They bumped and they shoved.

But the cabbage did not move.

It did not even budge.

Fox and Hare jogged down the lane. They stopped when they saw Moose, Bear, and Wolf sitting in Moose's garden. Fox and Hare went over in hopes of a glass of lemonade.

But then Fox and Hare saw the cabbage. It was a **big** cabbage. It was a **really big** cabbage. It was the **biggest** cabbage they had ever seen. "It's **huge!** It's **enormous!**" barked Fox. "Why, this is a GIANT cabbage! This is sure to win a prize at the fair!" said Hare, hopping up and down.

"We cannot lift this cabbage alone," said Moose.
"We will help you," promised Fox and Hare.

Moose grabbed hold of the cabbage.
Bear grabbed hold of the cabbage.
Wolf grabbed hold of the cabbage.
Fox grabbed hold of the cabbage.
Hare grabbed hold of the cabbage.

They pushed and they tugged.
They bumped and they shoved.
But the cabbage did not move.
It did not even budge.

Old Porcupine waddled along then. She saw her friends sitting in the middle of Moose's garden.

Old Porcupine's eyes were not as sharp as they used to be, but she soon saw the cabbage. It was a **big** cabbage. It was a **really big** cabbage. It was almost the **biggest** cabbage her old eyes had ever seen. "Say, that's a **pretty big** cabbage there. That GIANT cabbage could win a prize at the fair!" Porcupine said.

"We cannot lift this cabbage alone," complained Moose. "I will help you," promised Old Porcupine. "But first, we need some tools."

Old Porcupine sent Wolf to find her toolbox. Bear and Fox found wood for a ramp. Moose found a rope in his garden shed. Hare moved the truck closer. At last they were ready to try again.

Moose grabbed hold of the cabbage. Bear grabbed hold of the cabbage. Wolf grabbed hold of the cabbage. Fox grabbed hold of the cabbage. Hare grabbed hold of the cabbage. And Old Porcupine grabbed hold of the ends of the rope.

They pushed and they tugged.

They bumped and they shoved.

And the cabbage began to move,

but *only* a budge.

Squirrel scampered down from his tree to see what all the fuss was about.

He saw the cabbage. It was a **big** cabbage. It was a **really big** cabbage. It was the **biggest** cabbage he had ever seen. "It's **huge! It's enormous!**" Squirrel chattered. "Why, this is a GIANT cabbage! This is sure to win a prize at the fair!"

"Well, it might," Bear sighed, "but we have not been able to lift this cabbage."

"Have you tried a stick?" suggested Squirrel. "I use sticks to move rocks that cover my cache of nuts."

The animal friends thought this was a splendid idea.

"This may be just the thing we need to load this cabbage onto the truck," said Wolf, pulling over a strong branch.

Moose grabbed hold of the cabbage.
Bear grabbed hold of the cabbage.
Wolf grabbed hold of the cabbage.
Fox grabbed hold of the cabbage.
Hare grabbed hold of the cabbage.
Old Porcupine grabbed hold of the ends of the rope.
And Squirrel grabbed hold of the branch.

They pushed
and they tugged.
They bumped
and they shoved.
And the cabbage began
to move . . .
but only another budge.

"What we need is just a teeny,
tiny, little more of a push,"
insisted Old Porcupine.

"We're tired! We can't push any
harder," whined Fox.

But the animal friends would
not give up.

So they sat and they rested.

As the Midnight Sun moved across the sky, Little Vole poked her nose out of her burrow.

She saw the cabbage. It was a **big** cabbage. It was a **really big** cabbage. It was the **biggest** cabbage she had ever seen. "It's **huge!** It's **enormous!**" Vole squeaked. "Why, this is a GIANT cabbage! This is sure to win a prize at the fair!"

"Well, it might," Moose said, "but we cannot lift this cabbage."

"I will help you," promised Little Vole.

Moose grabbed hold of the cabbage.

Bear grabbed hold of the cabbage.

Wolf grabbed hold of the cabbage.

Fox grabbed hold of the cabbage.

Hare grabbed hold of the cabbage.

Old Porcupine grabbed hold of the ends of the rope.

Squirrel grabbed hold of the branch.

And Little Vole grabbed hold of the last teeny, tiny, little open spot on the cabbage's side.

They pushed and they tugged. They bumped and they shoved. Then they all pushed a little bit more.
    And the cabbage began to move up the ramp
                                        ever
                                            so
                                                slowly,
                                                    until . . .

KEEEEEEEEEEEEerWHUMP!

The GIANT cabbage landed with a thump and a bumpity-bump.

"HOORAY!" shouted the animals.

Then they sat down with a thump and a bumpity-bump.

"We did it!" panted Hare.

"Oh, thank you, my dear, dear friends!" cried Moose. "Now we can go to the fair!"

The animal friends scrambled into the truck and thumped and bumped down the road to the fair.

At the fair, the GIANT cabbage rolled slowly back down the ramp and landed with a thump and a bumpity-bump right in front of the judges.

The judges looked surprised. It was a **big** cabbage. It was a **really big** cabbage. It was the **biggest** cabbage they had ever seen. "It's **huge!** It's **enormous!**" they marveled. "Why, this GIANT cabbage wins the prize for the fair!"

"HOORAY!" shouted the animals again. "Let's go have fun at the fair!"

"Now we need to get all this fine cabbage home for our supper," said Moose.

"It's a good thing I brought Old Porcupine's tool box," said Wolf.

Soon, the GIANT cabbage was trimmed into a GIANT pile of cabbage pieces.

Moose and Bear grabbed hold of the extra-large pieces of cabbage.

Wolf and Fox grabbed hold of the large pieces of cabbage.

Hare and Old Porcupine grabbed hold of the medium pieces of cabbage.

Squirrel grabbed hold of a small piece of cabbage.

And Little Vole grabbed the last teeny, tiny, little piece of cabbage.

They pushed and they tugged.
They bumped and they shoved.
And they plopped the GIANT
cabbage pieces into the back of the truck.

Then Moose, Bear, Wolf, Fox and Hare, Old
Porcupine, Squirrel, and Little Vole scrambled
into the truck—and they thumped and bumped
back down the road to Moose's house.

"Let's make some cabbage soup," suggested Moose.

The animal friends ran home. Then they pushed and they tugged, they bumped and they shoved, and they brought things for the soup.

Moose dropped in the cabbage and stirred the pot.

Bear dropped in potatoes and stirred the pot.

Wolf dropped in squash and stirred the pot.

Fox and Hare dropped in onions and carrots
and stirred the pot.

Old Porcupine brought loaves
of her freshly baked bread.

Squirrel dropped in spices
and stirred the pot one more time.

And the dinner was complete
with a yummy berry treat
made by their own Little Vole.

The animals danced and sang while the giant soup pot bubbled.

Then they ate a wonderful meal of Moose's GIANT, and now prize-winning cabbage as they celebrated their friendship under the Midnight Sun.

(And there are still probably leftovers if you really want some!)

ALASKA VEGETABLES

The Matanuska-Susitna Valley, about 40 miles north of Anchorage, is famous for its huge vegetables, especially its giant cabbages. The vegetables grow so large because during the summer in Alaska, the days are very, very long. In fact, on June 21, the summer solstice, the Matanuska-Susitna Valley enjoys 19 hours and 44 minutes of daylight. With this "Midnight Sun," some garden vegetables get a great deal bigger in only one day!

The Matanuska-Susitna Valley is also home to the largest of the Alaska State Fairs, held each year at the end of August near Palmer. As in many state fairs, gardeners in Alaska compete for prizes awarded to the largest vegetables. At the Palmer Alaska State Fair, there has been a Giant Cabbage Contest since 1941. The current record for the largest cabbage, set in 2000, is 105.6 pounds. That's about the same as 3 second-graders, 6 mountain bikes, 29 six-packs of soda, 38 video game systems, or 400 Game Boys!

FOLKTALE

The story of the giant cabbage is based on a traditional Russian folktale about a turnip that is so big, the farmer can't pull it out of the ground without a lot of help. The story of the giant turnip has been retold in countless ways throughout the centuries. Yet no matter how the story changes, its message is always the same: Friends and family who work together can get any job done—and sometimes it's the tiniest of friends who make things happen. This is part of the spirit of Alaska.

MOOSE'S CABBAGE SOUP

Makes twelve 8-ounce servings

3 quarts chicken or vegetable stock

4 tablespoons (½ stick) butter

2 large onions, diced

1 large head of cabbage, quartered and chopped

1 pound unpeeled potatoes, cubed (use small red or yellow russet)

1 pound carrots, sliced in ¼-inch rounds (or cut baby carrots into thirds)

¼ cup dried parsley

2 tablespoons dried oregano

Salt and freshly ground pepper to taste

Water

Optional ingredients:

2 cans (14.5 ounces each) stewed tomatoes, well drained

3 cups fresh spinach leaves, washed and de-stemmed

1 bunch celery, cleaned and diced

1 large zucchini squash, cubed

In a GIANT soup pot, bring the stock to a boil.

In a 12-inch frying pan, melt the butter and sauté the onions until golden, about 5 minutes. Add to the soup pot, along with any butter remaining in the pan.

Add the remaining ingredients, including the optional ones of your choice, and cover the vegetables with water or additional stock. Simmer over low heat, stirring occasionally, until the carrots are soft and the potatoes are cooked, about 2 hours. Add salt and pepper to taste before serving.

Serve with a nice cheddar cheese, some crusty bread, and a good story.